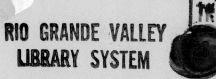

Matthew's Meadow

By Corinne Demas Bliss
Pictures by Ted Lewin

Jane Yolen Books
Harcourt Brace & Company
San Diego   New York   London

Requests for permission to make copies of any part of
the work should be mailed to: Permissions Department,
Harcourt Brace & Company, 8th Floor,
Orlando, Florida 32887.

Library of Congress Cataloging-in-Publication Data
Bliss, Corinne Demas.
Matthew's meadow/Corinne Demas Bliss; pictures by Ted Lewin.
p.   cm.
"Jane Yolen books."
Summary: Every year at blackberry time Matthew visits the red-tailed
hawk in the black walnut tree in the meadow, and she teaches him
how to use his senses to fully appreciate the natural world.
ISBN 0-15-200759-8
[1. Hawks—Fiction. 2. Senses and sensation—Fiction.
3. Nature—Fiction.]   I. Lewin, Ted, ill. II. Title.
PZ7.B61917Mat   1992
[E]—dc20   91-10840

B C D E F

Printed in Singapore

FOR *Austin* AND *Artemis*

— C. D. B.

For LOUIS AGASSIZ FUERTES,

who made birds speak to me

— T. L.

The illustrations in this book were done in watercolors
on D'Arches 300-lb. cold press watercolor paper.
The display and text type were set in ITC Garamond Book
by Thompson Type, San Diego, California.
Color separations were made by Bright Arts, Ltd., Singapore.
Printed and bound by Tien Wah Press, Singapore
Production supervision by Warren Wallerstein
and Ginger Boyer
Designed by Camilla Filancia

FAR UP ON THE HILL, far beyond where the eyes of the house could see, was a meadow of long, soft grass. A forest circled this meadow, and once this meadow had been forest, too. Someone had cleared the trees, leaving only one tree to grow tall in the center, a black walnut tree, taller than any tree around. The red-tailed hawk perched in this tree and looked out over the meadow and the whole hillside below.

This was Matthew's meadow, and he shared it with no one except the red-tailed hawk, and the deer who came there to sleep at night and at daybreak disappeared back into the woods. Matthew had never seen the deer because he had never been there at night. The meadow was far up the hillside, far from the house, far from his own room and his own bed. But he could see where the deer had flattened the grass when they slept and he could lie in the shallow hollows where they had lain.

This was Matthew's meadow because he thought of it as his, though he never told anyone about it. When his mother or father asked where he was off to, when his chores were done, he would say he was just going up the hill for a while. He went to his meadow when he wanted a place to think and when he wanted a place not to think at all. He would lie in the long, soft grass and watch the sky and watch the wind stirring the leaves of the black walnut tree. He would watch the red-tailed hawk survey the mountains and then fly off, to be lost, finally, in the sky.

One afternoon Matthew brought field glasses up to his meadow and focused on the red-tailed hawk who perched on a branch above him. The hawk looked right back at him and Matthew realized the hawk could see him just as well with her plain eyes. They stared at each other for a while and when Matthew put the field glasses down by his side the hawk spoke up.

"I surprise you," said the hawk, "but that's to be expected. Soon you will get used to my voice and you won't find it strange that I speak to you, that we speak with each other."

Matthew knew, just as you do, that birds and animals speak in stories but that real life is a different thing. Matthew is part of this story now, but, when the story took place, he was as real as you are. So of course he was amazed to hear the hawk speak. But very quickly, and without knowing why, he

forgot his amazement. And soon the hawk's voice seemed as natural to him as his own.

"Do you know how this meadow came to be here?" asked the hawk.

"No," said Matthew. The meadow had been there for as long as he could remember. He thought it had always been there.

"Your grandmother made this meadow for you. The black walnut tree has kept the forest back, as black walnut trees do, but it was she who cleared out the brambles and the bushes, and she who planted the grass. She wanted you to have a place in the forest where you could see the sky."

"Is she there?" asked Matthew. "Is she there in the sky?" As he said this he felt it was a silly question, a question he would have asked when he was a little child. Matthew's grandmother had died when he was just old enough to remember her. She had been buried, he knew, in the cemetery in town. But when he thought of her, and he thought of her often when he came up to his meadow, he liked to think of her somewhere up in the sky, watching him from a cloud.

"If that's where you like to think of her," said the red-tailed hawk, "then that's where she is."

"Do you know?" asked Matthew. "How do you know?"

The hawk flew down and perched on the lowest branch of the black walnut tree. She was the closest she had ever been.

"There are things that I can tell you," said the hawk, "and there are things that I can't. There are things I will tell you that you won't understand until you are older, and there are some things you may never understand. And if you don't understand something you must try to think about it for a year before you ask me to explain."

Matthew said he would. He stood up very quietly. The red-tailed hawk was preening her feathers. She looked just like a bird, a bird who could not speak, and for a moment

Matthew thought that the voice must have been in a dream, in his mind. As if she had heard Matthew's doubts, the hawk looked down at him and asked loudly, "How old are you?"

"Nine," said Matthew. "I just turned nine."

"Can you remember today?" asked the hawk. "Can you remember to be here this day next year?"

"I think so," said Matthew. "I'll try."

"Go to the edge of the meadow," said the hawk, "where the blackberry bushes grow. See if they can help you."

Matthew ran through the grass to the edge of the meadow where the wild blackberries grew. They had just turned from deep red to the color of crows, and they came off easily in his hand. A few days before, they had held on to the stem.

"Next year," said the hawk, "blackberry time."

"Next year," repeated Matthew, "blackberry time."

"Come back here next year and I'll have something to teach you. Come back here every year at blackberry time and you will learn something new. And when you are old enough to understand things for yourself you will find a way to let your grandmother know what you learned. For the things that I will tell you all come from her."

"From her?" asked Matthew. "Did you speak with her, too?"

"Many years ago," said the red-tailed hawk, "when you were just a baby, your grandmother carried you up here to show you to me. She was not an ordinary woman, your grandmother; she knew many special things, and she wanted you to know them, too. She asked me to teach you these things as you grew older, because she knew she would not be alive to teach them to you herself."

"How did she know I would talk to you?" asked Matthew.

"How did she know you would make this your meadow?" asked the hawk, and she flew off, leaving her question as the answer.

And now, you must wonder: what did Matthew say when he came down from his meadow and went back to his house? Although birds can talk to children in the real world, that's not something grown-ups would ever believe. Matthew walked down the hillside, eating blackberries, and by the time he got home he did not remember that the hawk had spoken. He remembered what the hawk had said, but he thought they were his own words, inside his head. He thought he had come to know all this while he was in his meadow watching the sky by himself.

Exactly a year later, when Matthew was ten, he went up the hill to his meadow. He brought his scythe with him, as he sometimes did, to keep the meadow clear, and he brought a basket, too. Three days before, the blackberries had not been quite ripe enough to pick, but this day they came off easily in his hand. As he was picking he began to think that there was something he should remember.

"Blackberry time," he said to himself, "blackberry time."

He took his half-filled basket and went to lie in the long, soft grass at the foot of the black walnut tree. He lay back in the grass and looked up at the sky and watched the fat, white clouds move past like floats in a parade. Then he noticed a familiar shape against the sun. When he shaded his eyes he saw the red-tailed hawk watching him from a branch above and he felt a burst of excitement. Now, a red-tailed hawk is a magnificent sight to see, just on its own, but Matthew knew, though he was not sure why, there was more to it than that. When the hawk spoke he was not surprised.

"Hello," said the hawk, as if she had expected Matthew to turn up. "I have a job for you to do."

Matthew stood up.

"Go find a milkweed pod that survived the winter," said the hawk, "and bring it back here."

Matthew knew that the milkweed grew at one side of the meadow. The monarch larvae lived on milkweed, and at the end of summer the plump yellow-striped caterpillars turned into pupae there, and then into butterflies that flew off for the winter. The milkweed was green again, the monarchs were back, but Matthew was able to find an old pod that was still sealed.

"Open it very carefully," said the hawk, "and let out just a few seeds, one at a time."

Matthew cracked open the pod of the milkweed along its seam. The seeds, with their silky white threads, were packed tight, and Matthew knew they would billow out like feathers from a ripped pillow. He plucked out a few strands, and as soon as he

opened his palm the wind lifted them into the air and carried them off toward the sky.

"A few more," said the hawk, "and listen to them this time."

Matthew bent toward the milkweed pod and nudged a few more seeds away from the pack. They took off quickly into space.

"I don't hear anything, " he said to the hawk.

"Try again," said the hawk. "Close off all your other senses, if you have to, but open yourself to listening. Become your ears."

Matthew tried again. He put his ear close to the milkweed

and he thought about listening. He closed himself off from
the sight of the blue sky and the fat, white clouds. He closed
himself off from the taste of blackberries in his mouth and the
feel of the sun on his arms. And he listened as hard as he could.

And then, slowly, as each seed lifted into space, he
began to hear them. At first what he heard was the sound
of the wind. But the hawk told him to listen better. Matthew
listened so hard he became his ears, and soon he could hear
the sound of each milkweed seed as it lost its grip on the
cluster and flew off, perhaps to become a milkweed plant of
its own. And each milkweed seed made a beautiful sweet
sound, like a note from a harp.

"Now you know how to really listen," said the hawk. "There are things to hear that you've never thought to listen to before. Everything in nature has its own sound. Listen to things move, listen to things grow, listen to things change. Listen to stillness. In the winter, when it snows, you will discover that even each snowflake has its own sound."

"Will I remember all this when winter comes?" asked Matthew.

"Did you remember to come here at blackberry time?" asked the hawk, and she flew off. Matthew was not surprised. He had learned that questions can be answers, too.

When he came down from the mountain, carrying his half-filled basket, Matthew remembered what the hawk had taught him, but he did not remember that it was the hawk who had been his teacher. He thought he had come to know these things by himself.

And during the year, he found that he could hear things he had never heard before. When he listened he was able

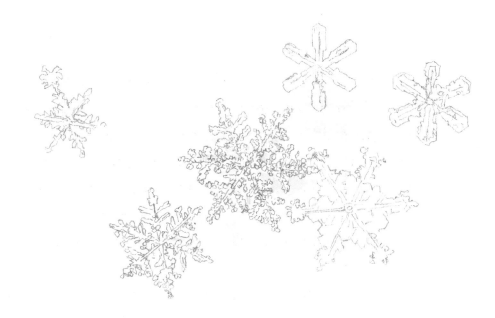

to hear the sound of the smallest insect making its way
along the stem of a plant. He could hear the sound of toads
moving through the grass, and the sound of water moving
underground, and the sound of leaves dying as winter
came, and the sound of the earth beginning to freeze.
In the winter, when it snowed, he listened to the snow and
he discovered the secret of snowflakes. He had known
that every snowflake has a different shape, but now
he found that each snowflake falling made a
different sound, like the chime of a miniature bell,
and that together the snowflakes
sounded like a carillon.

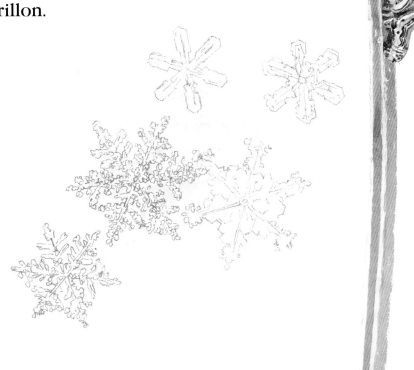

At the same time the next year, when Matthew was
eleven, he went up to his meadow. He knew there was a
special reason for him to be there, but he was not sure what
it was.

He lay in the long, soft grass, eating blackberries, and
listening to the clouds move in the sky. When he looked up
into the black walnut tree and saw the red-tailed hawk, he
remembered instantly why he was there.

"Can you listen now?" asked the hawk. "Can you hear the smallest things?"

"Yes," said Matthew. "I can hear the water lilies on the pond close up when evening comes. I can hear the dew dry from the grass."

"And the snowflakes," asked the hawk, "can you hear them?"

"Every one," said Matthew.

"Good," said the hawk. "You have learned how to listen. This time, I'd like to teach you something new. Stand up and tell me, can you feel the wind?"

Matthew stood up in the grass and faced into the light wind. His hair blew back from his face and his shirt moved against his skin.

"Yes," he said, "I feel the wind."

"Now," said the hawk, "I want you to feel the wind on your forehead alone. And then I want you to feel the wind on your cheeks. And then I want you to tilt up your chin and feel the wind on your neck."

Matthew held his face into the wind and felt it touch his forehead, then his cheeks, then his neck.

"Now," said the hawk, "hold out your hand and turn it slowly. I want you to feel the wind on your palm, and then I want you to feel each finger in the wind, one at a time. The wind on your forehead is different from the wind on your cheeks. Even each finger feels different in the wind."

Matthew held out his hand and felt the wind brush across the top, then the palm. The hawk counted off his fingers as he held them out into the wind, one by one.

"Now," said the hawk, "I want you to forget about the wind. I want you to think about the sun. Hold your face to the sun, and then hold out your hand."

Matthew thought about the sun on his forehead and his cheeks. He tilted his chin and felt the sun on his neck. Then he turned his hand in the sun and felt it on his fingers one by one.

"Your skin is not a shell to hold all of you inside," said the hawk. "Your skin is like a million windows, open to touch. This year you'll learn about how much there is to feel, just as last year you learned how much there was to listen to."

"Will you be here next year? Again?" asked Matthew.

"Will you come to your meadow at blackberry time?" asked the hawk, and she left her question behind her as she flew off.

When Matthew came down from the meadow, he remembered what the hawk had taught him, but he did not remember that it was the hawk who had been his teacher. He thought he had come to know these things by himself. All year long he felt things he had never felt before; the world had a new texture for him. When he swam in the pond he found that the water on his shoulder felt different from the water on his belly and the water on his toes. In winter he felt the differences between snowflakes as each one landed on his face. At night he could feel the moonlight as it touched him and the starlight that tingled on his skin. He could feel the blood chugging through his body and he could feel the thoughts churning in his mind.

For the next four years, just at blackberry time, Matthew came up to the meadow and found the red-tailed hawk waiting for him in the black walnut tree. And each year the hawk taught him something new.

When Matthew was twelve he learned how to smell where the deer had lain. He could smell a rainstorm far away and he could smell the coming of night.

When Matthew was thirteen he learned to taste all the intricacies of an apple. He could taste one blackberry from another.

When Matthew was fourteen the hawk taught him to notice things that were too small for him to have noticed before, and to take in things that had been too big. He could observe the habits of mites and comprehend the curvature of the earth. The hawk taught him how to watch for changes

that had been too slow for him to see before, like the erosion of the mountains, and to watch movements that passed too quickly for him, like the beating of a hummingbird's wings. His eyes could follow the progress of the stone that he sent skipping across the surface of the pond as if it were in slow motion.

When Matthew was fifteen, the hawk showed him that the eyes inside his mind — his memory and his imagination — saw more than the eyes of his face, and the hawk taught him how to use those eyes together. So when Matthew looked at a leaf he could see its underside as well. And he could see, with

his memory, how the leaf had looked before it had unfolded into green, when it was first formed, tightly wrapped. And with the help of his imagination he could see it as it would become, turning to a hot orange in the fall, exhausting itself in color, and then falling brown and brittle to the ground. The hawk taught him that his memory could store all his senses as well, so that in addition to seeing, he could feel and smell and taste and hear what he wanted to, right in his mind.

All of these things he learned from the hawk, but he did not remember that it was the hawk who had taught him. He thought that he had come to learn these things, in his meadow, on his own.

When Matthew was sixteen he went up to his meadow at blackberry time, just as he had the seven years before. As

Matthew had gotten older, the hawk had gotten older, too. She seemed smaller to Matthew, just as the meadow seemed smaller and the black walnut tree seemed smaller. Only the sky hadn't changed. It was just as immense, just as far away, just as elusive as the life before he had been born.

Matthew lay on his back in the long, soft grass and looked up at the red-tailed hawk. And although he did not remember to expect it, when the hawk began to speak, he was not surprised. The hawk's voice was weaker than it had ever been, and Matthew stood up to hear her better.

"Now," said the hawk, "your five senses are fully awake. You know all the secrets that your grandmother asked me to reveal to you. You are sixteen. You're on the brink of becoming a man. Today I want to tell you about one last thing, something that comes from me, something that will help you in the years ahead."

Matthew suddenly felt sadness move through him. He heard, in his mind, a coming farewell.

"I wish you could speak to my grandmother now," said Matthew. "I wish you could tell her that I learned what she wanted me to learn. I wish you could thank her for me."

"That," said the hawk, "is something you'll have to do yourself."

"How can I?" asked Matthew.

"When you were a little child," said the hawk, "all kinds of things seemed possible. As you got older and wiser you

learned more and more about the boundaries of your world, and you got more and more used to thinking within those boundaries. The unknown is simply the not-yet-known.

Most people look for solutions within the known. If this is something you want to do, and you think it is impossible, I want you to look outside the known, not within it. I want you to learn to think beyond your thoughts."

Matthew had always listened unquestioningly to the red-tailed hawk. But he was older now. Although it was not the first time that the hawk's ideas had puzzled him, it was the first time he spoke up.

"You've always talked in riddles," said Matthew. "Although I never remembered you were my teacher, in time what you said made sense. Now I don't understand you at all."

"How long did I ask you to think about the things I said?"

"A year," said Matthew. "And in a year I learned."

"What I told you today is much harder to understand," said the hawk. "Ten times harder. So it will take you ten times as long. Put it away in a back pocket of your mind and take it out now and then and turn it over when you have a chance. And in ten years come back up to your meadow —"

"In ten years —" began Matthew.

"You'll be grown up completely by then," said the hawk, "you'll be a man."

But that wasn't what Matthew wanted to ask.

"Will you —?" he began.

"Can you watch me?" asked the hawk. "Can you watch me even when you can't see me anymore?" She pushed off from her branch and sailed up into the sky, circling and soaring higher and farther away. Matthew watched as her shape grew indistinct, and watched as she became just a tiny,

dark spot, and watched her in his mind when she was too far
away for him to see her with his eyes.

Matthew came sadly down from his meadow and walked
across the fields to his house. In his mind he listened to the
words "think beyond your thoughts," but he did not know
where they had come from and he did not know what they
meant. He put them in a back pocket of his mind, and now
and then he would take them out and turn them over and over
again.

The next year, when blackberry time came, Matthew was
seventeen. He was too old to be interested in picking berries.

He was busy working in the fields. He did not go up to his meadow at blackberry time in the coming years, but he went there at other times to watch the sky and to think his thoughts and to not think at all.

He knew that it was in the meadow, when he was a boy, that his senses had awakened, one by one. He remembered the red-tailed hawk who used to perch above him in the black walnut tree, but he did not remember that the hawk had spoken with him, that it was the hawk who had taught him how to really listen, feel, smell, taste, and see.

As Matthew grew up he started taking over more and more of the work on his parents' farm, and when they got older they turned the farm over to him. He was a good farmer, because they had taught him all about the land. But he felt it was from his grandmother, though he didn't understand how, that he had learned about himself. He felt that somehow, in the meadow she had cleared for him, he had discovered all the things she had wanted him to learn, and he wished he could find a way to let her know, and to thank her for these gifts. For his life, although much of it was spent alone, was a very rich one. He could listen to his hay growing. He could feel the pattern of sun on his hands. He could smell evening move across his fields. He could remember the tastes of the cornbread he had eaten at breakfast. He could see the face of the girl whom he was beginning to care for. And more and more often he took out the words "think beyond your thoughts," from the back pocket of his mind and turned them over and over again.

When Matthew was twenty-six years old, he went up
again to his meadow at blackberry time, carrying his baby
daughter. The meadow seemed small to him, just a grassy
plot, and the black walnut tree seemed no taller than the trees
in the forest around it. But when he looked up at the sky it
seemed as immense as it had when he was a little boy. And
as he watched the fat, white clouds move across the sky
he remembered how, as a child, he used to think that his
grandmother was somewhere in the sky, watching him from
a cloud. More than ever before, he wanted to reach out to

her, through time, through space, and tell her what he had learned. As he thought of her, he thought about the red-tailed hawk and for the first time he remembered that the red-tailed hawk had actually spoken to him.

There was no red-tailed hawk perched in the black walnut tree this blackberry time; there was no red-tailed hawk circling high overhead. But Matthew could see her clearly with the eyes inside his mind. He could see her circling in the sky and at the same time he could see her on a branch overhead, and in his mind he could hear the hawk's voice, which was as clear as the first time she had spoken.

"The unknown," said the hawk, "is simply the not-yet-known. Think beyond your thoughts so that you can find a way to do what you once thought impossible."

Matthew lay in the long, soft grass, his baby asleep in his arms. In his mind he watched the red-tailed hawk coast across the sky, and he began, slowly, to think beyond his thoughts.

He began to wander in a region where his mind had never wandered before, and there he discovered something he hadn't known. He hadn't known it because he had been thinking in words, and this was an idea that came to him not in words but some other way.

There was, he realized, a language of the land. It was there in nature, in the way the mountains grew and eroded, in the way the stream meandered. The earth was — when you looked at it and touched it and listened to it — its own design. The meadow his grandmother had cleared for him gave him the forest and the sky. Gave him the black walnut tree and the red-tailed hawk. His grandmother had spoken to him through the land. He, too, could speak to her through the land itself.

And so, when Matthew came down from his meadow, he began his message. The trees that he planted, the pond that he banked, the fields that he tilled, were the way he spoke. From the sky above the message was clear; but the message went underground, into the earth, as well. As he worked through the language of the land, he told his grandmother the story of his life. He told her how he had learned from her. He thanked her and told her of his love.

And when Matthew smelled the coming of spring and listened to the blackberries grow, and saw in his mind the red-tailed hawk perched in the black walnut tree, which towered over his meadow as it had when he was a boy, he knew that she had heard.